Praise for ... BROCK, PIKE & ROOK

"Never have three sparsely written novellas packed such an emotional punch. Not a word is wasted and, for me, they are the absolute definition of the word 'classic'" PHIL EARLE, *GUARDIAN*

"Gritty, unflinching and authentic ... with a life-affirming warmth" CARNEGIE JUDGING PANEL ON *ROOK*

"McGowan ... freights every word with truth and feeling ... Few other writers for the young better understand the pull of the gang and the fear of the bully" *TIMES* ON *BROCK*

"A gut-wrenching tale of crime and punishment makes [*Pike*] compelling reading" *NEW STATESMAN* ON *PIKE*

"Lucid and sharp as broken glass, it's a book filled with raw, elemental emotion" *GUARDIAN* ON *ROOK*

"[Nature] provides a moment of epiphany that resounds. Simply told, yet laced with urgency, this will spellbind" PHILIP WOMACK, *DAILY TELEGRAPH*, ON *BROCK*

"An uncondescending and atmospheric novella" CBI ON *BROCK*

"Dazzlingly true to life, a succinct yet satisfying read" *INIS* ON *PIKE*

"McGowan writes in prose as spare and effective as that of Barry Hines ... there's an extraordinary depth and elegance to this story. An outstanding novel" ANDREA REECE, LOVEREADING4KIDS ON *PIKE*

"*Rook* is an outstanding piece of writing ... unflinching and authentic, funny and grit   y bookshe

LARK

Anthony McGowan

Barrington Stoke

First published in 2019 in Great Britain by
Barrington Stoke Ltd
18 Walker Street, Edinburgh, EH3 7LP

www.barringtonstoke.co.uk

A CIP catalogue record for this book is available
from the British Library upon request

ISBN: 978-1-78112-843-5

Printed in China by Leo

This book has dyslexia-friendly features

To Mairi Kidd, who mothered my boys

Prologue

"I don't bloody like it."

"Language, Kenny," I said to my brother. "You don't have to bloody well say bloody all the bloody time. It's not clever, and it's not funny."

I copied the whining voice of Mr Kimble, our English teacher. But it was wasted on Kenny, as he didn't go to my school.

"But it is bloody cold," Kenny said.

"I know."

"And we're bloody lost."

"I bloody know."

I looked around. It had stopped snowing, but the path had almost vanished. I saw white fields and stone walls. The black skeletons of trees climbing out of the frozen earth. The sky was a sort of pale grey, like a seagull's back. In fact, the sky was the weirdest thing about it all. You couldn't see any clouds, or any of the blue in between the clouds. Just this solid grey nothing like cold porridge, going on for ever.

I had Tina, our Jack Russell, on the lead. She'd enjoyed the snow to begin with, snapping at it and chewing mouthfuls, as if she'd caught a rat. But now she looked as fed up as us. She was getting on a bit, and the cold had got into her bones.

"And there's worser words than bloody," Kenny said. He had his big hands thrust into the pockets of his jeans to hide them from the wind. "There's this boy, Milo, at school, and he knows all of them."

"What?" I snorted. "He knows every bad word there is?"

"Yeah."

"What, every bad word in the whole world?"

"Yeah, course," Kenny said. "Well, maybe not in the world, but in England. Cos, yeah, there might be bad words in other countries he doesn't know, like the Chinese for knob and the African for arse."

"African isn't a language, Kenny," I told him. "It's not even a country. There are loads of countries in Africa and hundreds of languages. They all have mucky words in them."

"Whatever," Kenny said, getting annoyed. But at least his mind wasn't on the snow and the cold and the mess we were in.

"Go on then," I said.

"What?"

"These bad words Milo told you, let's hear them."

"You won't tell Dad or Jenny that I know them?" Kenny asked.

"Course not. I'm not a grass."

"You told them where I hid the turkey."

"I had to," I said. "Otherwise there'd have been no Christmas dinner."

Kenny nodded. He could see the logic in that.

"OK, then," Kenny said. "Right ..."

And then Kenny told me all the dirty words he knew. It made us laugh, but not enough to warm us up. Half of the words weren't even real. Stuff like "splonger" and "bozzle". I don't know if this Milo kid had said it for a joke, or if someone had told him that nonsense and he just passed it on.

The best was when Kenny said, "A sod, do you know what that is?"

"Not really," I replied.

"It's one of the worst words there is," Kenny told me. "Even saying it gets you a million years in hell. A sod is a man who digs up dead bodies to have it off with."

"I'm not sure it is, Kenny," I said, spluttering.

"It is! And a daft sod is one who forgets his spade."

And then I laughed so hard I cried, and snot came out of my nose. The tears and snot were warm for a moment on my skin, and then cold, cold.

"You, you're a daft sod," I said.

Kenny shoved me, and I was laughing too much to keep my balance and I fell over. Tina got excited for the first time in ages and barked and scampered around.

I hit the ground and felt the snow under me, and under the snow the hardness of the frozen earth. Then I realised just how much trouble we were in.

I stood up and brushed off the snow. I think Kenny was expecting me to push him back, so he was laughing but keeping his distance. Then Kenny saw my face, and he stopped laughing.

"We better get off this hill, Kenny," I said. "Or we'll catch our bloody deaths."

One

It wasn't supposed to be like this. It was meant to be a stroll, a laugh.

A lark.

It was our dad's idea. Kenny had been bored and excited at the same time for a while now, and that made him act up a lot. Sometimes he sulked, not saying anything for hours. He'd stare at the rain running down the windows as if he was watching the telly. And then something would set him off and he'd go manic. He'd punch the cushions on the settee or shout out random stuff in the street or scramble to the top of the climbing frame in the park and howl like a wolf. That made the kids playing there laugh, but it freaked out the mums and dads and child-minders smoking on the broken benches.

Kenny was bored because it was the Easter holidays and none of his mates were around. He went to a special school, and the kids travelled there from all over the place. None of them lived near us.

He was excited because next week our mum was coming to visit us from Canada. She left us when we were little, and we hadn't seen her since. It turned out that she'd sent letters and cards every birthday. But we moved so many times, flitting from paying the rent, that they never reached us. And then she finally tracked us down.

She was coming to stay – not with us, but in a hotel. She couldn't stay with us because my dad had a new girlfriend, Jenny, and it would have messed with Jenny's head.

So that's why Kenny had been bored and excited.

And he wasn't the only one.

I was just as messed up about our mum coming as Kenny, but I'd got good at hiding my feelings. Years ago, I'd hidden my feelings about my mum and everything for Kenny's sake. But after a while, it gets to be a habit. You keep the feelings on the inside, like the way you hide a sweet in your mouth in lessons at school. Except the feelings aren't sweet.

And there was another thing I wanted to stop thinking about. I'd had a girlfriend, and then I didn't. I couldn't talk about it to Kenny or my dad or Jenny. It was a sick feeling inside me all the time, like when you've eaten something a bit off.

So, yeah, I was in a state, too, and when my dad said I should take Kenny up for a walk on the moors, I was well up for it.

"It's nice up there," Dad said. We were sitting in the kitchen, having a cup of tea. Dad had just come home from a long night shift and looked knackered. "Your granddad used to take me up on the moors when I was a nipper, before he got sick," Dad told me. "And it's not like now, when you see people going for a stroll all kitted out as if they're off to the South Pole. All we'd bring was a carrier bag with a bottle of pop in it and some jam sandwiches. And we'd walk until we got somewhere high, so you could see all the world below you – the fields and woods and hills. Until in the distance your eyes came to a dirty smudge, and that was Leeds."

My dad didn't talk much about his mum and dad. They'd died before me and Kenny were born.

Granddad had been a miner, like my dad was before they shut the pits and everyone lost their jobs.

My dad was looking into the distance now, not across the fields but back. Back to the hill and the moors, and the pop and the jam sandwiches, and *his* dad.

After a couple of seconds, he went on, "At this time of year the larks will be singing."

"What's larks?" asked Kenny, who'd just burst into the kitchen.

"A lark is a bird," I said.

I was good on birds. I knew what a lark was and what it looked like from pictures in books, but I'd never seen one in real life.

"Aye, that's right," Dad said. "They used to be dead common in the fields round here, but you don't see 'em any more."

"Why not?" Kenny asked. "Did someone kill 'em all?" Kenny may not have known what a lark was, but he loved animals and hated the thought of hurting them.

"Eh?" Dad said. "No, not really. The farmers changed the way they do things, so there's not as much for the larks to eat, especially in the winter. But back then, in spring and summer, you'd be walking down the lanes and all around you the larks would be shooting up straight into the sky like little brown fireworks. They'd sing their hearts out as they climbed – the dads showing off to the mams."

I looked at Kenny. His eyes were shining as he saw the larks soaring up into the blue sky of his mind. He loved fireworks more than anything. He was probably imagining the larks with sparks flying out of their arses.

So that's when we decided we'd go for a day up on the moors. Dad helped us plan it all out. "I know just the place to go," he said. We found it on Google Maps, and Dad printed it out. But the ink was running out, so the map was faded and blurry. We had to catch three buses to get there, changing at York and then at Thirsk. I liked the idea of getting three buses. It made it seem more like an adventure.

"You get off the last bus here," Dad said as he pointed it out on the map laid on the kitchen table. "There's a nice little lane." His finger traced a line that curved across the fields, joining up two villages. "It's only a couple of miles. There'll be shops and stuff there if you need extra supplies."

He jabbed again at the map. "You can pick up the bus back home from here."

We had to set off early, or we'd never get there and back in a day. My dad worked nights, wheeling sick people around on trolleys at the hospital. We'd have to get going before he got home. Normally, Jenny would have been there to help us sort everything out, but she was working shifts, too. So that morning it was just me and Kenny.

He'd woken up when it was still dark, the way he always did when something good was going to happen.

"Get up, our Nicky," Kenny yelled at me, and ruined a perfectly good dream I was having. Tina, who always slept with her bum in Kenny's face, picked up on the excitement and started barking and yapping.

Tina had a body the colour of a dirty hanky, and a brown face. She wasn't a genius, but she was loyal, and she'd have died for Kenny. We got her after she'd been left for dead by some bad lads. They'd been using her to hunt badgers. I suppose we'd saved Tina's life, and she thought she owed us.

"You feed Tina, then make the sandwiches," I told Kenny, "while I get the kit sorted."

"What sandwiches shall I do?" Kenny asked.

"Jam of course," I said, thinking of my dad and granddad back in the olden days. "And cheese. Do cheese as well."

I crammed some gloves and a scarf and an extra jumper and a bobble hat in my Adidas school bag, because I knew Kenny would have gone out without them. The scarf and the hat were in the Leeds United colours – white with yellow and blue stripes. I had the printed-out map and my phone was charged up. And I packed my good penknife in case we had to do some emergency stick-whittling or fight off zombies.

And I took a lighter as well, cramming it in my inside pocket. Just a cheap plastic one. I couldn't remember where it had come from. My dad didn't smoke. Sometimes I wondered if it had belonged to my mum. That's why I kept it, even though it had probably just been left behind by one of my dad's mates back when Dad was drinking all the time.

Two

The first bus left our town just before 8 a.m. That's the one we were meant to be on. We missed it. The next bus was at 9. We missed that one, too. We got to the stop in plenty of time, but then at the last minute Kenny remembered that he had to bring some treats for Tina. He ran back to the house and didn't get back before the bus went. So we got the 10 a.m. bus. While we were waiting, I had time to go to the Spar and get a giant bottle of no-name cola and some biscuits – chocolate digestives, Kenny's favourites.

"We'll have to march double quick when we're on the moors," I said to Kenny. "Or we'll be stuck out there when it gets dark."

Kenny carried Tina on to the bus while I paid our fares. Kenny liked to sit upstairs at the front of the bus. He used to pretend to drive it, stretching his arms out like he was holding the big steering wheel and making *brrrrum-brrrrum* bus noises. But he'd stopped doing that now. Or at least he'd stopped doing it on the outside. I think he still drove the bus in his mind, guiding it round the corners and slamming on the brakes if an old lady was at a zebra crossing.

Tina sat in between us, her tongue dangling out of her mouth. She liked an adventure even more than Kenny. My dad had said we had to keep her on the lead when we got off the bus, otherwise she'd be eating lamb chops while they were still part of the lamb. Sometimes Tina looked out of the window and sometimes she looked at Kenny. When she looked at Kenny, you knew that all she was thinking was the doggy version of "I love this". And maybe, "I love you".

It was meant to be spring, and when we started out it was like any other normal day – a bit dreary and grey, but not that bad. There was even the odd flash of blue in between the clouds. But the sky looked heavier and angrier every time I looked out of the window. The snow began to fall as the third of our three buses climbed up onto the moors.

"Snowing!" Kenny said, his eyes wide with wonder.

"Don't get excited," I said. "It won't set. It never does."

But I was wrong.

First the snow was really just rain with big ideas, melting the second it hit the windows of the bus. Then it was wet flakes that turned to slush on the road. And then the snowflakes became smaller and blew around in the wind. But when the snow landed on the fields beyond the stone walls, it stayed.

We were sat on the three buses for two and a half hours in total. It sounds boring, but it wasn't, not really. There was always something new to look at, and Kenny being happy made me feel happy, too. We ate the biscuits and drank half the cola. A few people chatted to us and asked where we were going. Old ladies, mainly, in big coats and hats. It was mostly me that replied. Kenny was shy. When we were kids, sometimes other kids would shout names at him, and so that made him wary. But old people were normally nice.

One lady had a dog – a fluffy white girl dog with a tartan coat and a pink ribbon. Tina was sometimes grumpy with other dogs, and she'd have a go at any that were bigger than her. But she got on OK with this fluffy one, and they sniffed noses.

"She's old, your Tina," the lady said as she got off the bus. "You want to get her a coat for the cold weather."

"Not Tina," I said. "She's a proper Yorkshire dog, tough as old boots."

The third bus was nearly empty by the time we got off.

"Where you two lads off to, then?" the driver asked us as the doors opened with a sigh. He was one of those little fat men that you always think is going to be jolly and friendly. But this one's face was all screwed up as if he'd just bitten into a bad pie. I suppose there must be a lot of pressure on you to be jolly when you look like a Christmas pudding with legs. You'd need to be strong to resist all that and still be grumpy.

"We're off to see larks," Kenny said. "We've got cheese and jam sandwiches. And pop."

"Aye, well, watch yourselves," the driver replied. "It's gonna be filthy up top."

He used a fat finger to point up towards the treeless hills.

"You're not dressed for it, neither," he added.

"We'll be fine," I said. "There's a footpath."

The bus driver nodded. "Stick to it."

Three

The footpath was a five-minute walk from the bus stop. You couldn't miss it. There was a stone wall with a gap in it, and a green sign that said PUBLIC FOOTPATH, just like my dad had told us.

I had a funny feeling as we left the road and started out on the path. One second there were cars and lorries thundering by, and the next you were in a different world. The stone walls were like the remains of ruined castles, and the black trees were monsters, frozen by the spells of a good wizard. It was almost like when you start reading a book, and from the moment you open it, you live there and not in the real world.

There was no sign of a lark. The only birds we saw were big black crows flying slowly and alone over the fields.

"I thought we might see Rooky," Kenny said.

Kenny was talking about the rook we'd rescued from getting eaten by a sparrowhawk last year. We'd cared for it for a while, then taken it to an animal refuge. We were there when they released it back into the wild. It was the second animal we'd saved. The year before that we looked after a baby badger. Caring for the animals probably helped us more than it helped them.

"I think it's a bit bleak up here for rooks," I said. "They're softies, really. Rooks like it down on the farms where the fields get ploughed and there's lots of beetles and worms for them. Up here is crow country."

"I don't like crows," Kenny said. "They always look pissed off."

"Yeah," I agreed. "And it always sounds like they're telling you to get lost."

The path climbed steadily, so you were always a bit out of breath but not enough to feel knackered. Our feet crunched over the snow, making a sound like you were eating biscuits.

The trees and hedges lined the path at the start and kept the wind off. But after twenty minutes we'd left most of the trees behind and were up on the high moor. That's when it really began to

feel cold. Partly it was because what was left of
the warmth from the bus had seeped away, but
mainly it was because of the wind. It was one of
those clever winds that knows how to get into you,
sneaking under your collar and up your sleeves.

I got the hat and gloves and scarf out of the bag
and held them out to Kenny.

"Put these on," I said.

Kenny hated hats and gloves and scarves. I
don't know why.

"You put 'em on. I'm not cold."

It was impossible to get Kenny to do anything
he didn't want to. Well, you could bribe him,
sometimes. But you couldn't force him. And
I couldn't have made him, anyway. He was as
scrawny as a streak of piss, but he was strong,
with hands like spades and big bony feet. When we
were kids, I could always beat him in a play fight by
tickling him, and he'd beg me to stop before he wet
himself. But now he always pinned me down before
I could get anywhere near his skinny ribs.

"Fine," I said.

And the truth is that it felt good having the hat
and gloves and scarf on. Like getting a cuddle from
your ... Well, like getting a cuddle.

Four

So me and Kenny chatted, and Tina had a sniff at everything that could be sniffed. And she peed on almost anything that stuck up out of the snow until she had no more pee left in her.

"Never eat yellow snow," I said to Kenny.

"I'm not gonna," Kenny said. "If it was really cold, would your piss freeze in mid-air?"

"I don't know. I suppose so. Yeah, hang on, I remember watching something on the telly about Siberia, or somewhere like that. A man poured boiling water out of a kettle and before it reached the ground it had turned to ice. So that must mean your piss would, too."

"I'd like to see that," Kenny said. "Your piss turning to ice in mid-air ..."

"But your willy would freeze and snap off like an icicle if you got it out in Siberia," I told him.

"It wouldn't!" Kenny said, horrified.

"Would, definitely. If it was a clean break, they could probably sew your willy back on again. Or superglue it."

"Superglue's rubbish," Kenny said. "Dad tried to glue the bottom of my shoe back on and it just fell off again. It doesn't stick anything together, apart from your fingers."

"Exactly," I said. "Fingers and willies – that's all it's good for."

That was the sort of chat we had, and it was a laugh, for a while.

The footpath was pretty easy to follow, despite the fact that the snow covered everything. There were stone walls on both sides, and even when there weren't, the path had its own shape, different to the fields around us. There was a high bit in the middle of the path, and then a lower bit on each side, and then high again at the edges. It looked like tyre tracks, but it might just have been from thousands of feet walking over it for hundreds of years.

Here and there we'd see sheep huddling against the field walls or spot their mucky arses as they ran away from us. Well, I suppose they were really running away from Tina, who barked and growled at them.

I don't know how much damage she could have done to the sheep, but she definitely wanted to have a go. I don't think dogs really know how big they are. I read that the only animals that can recognise themselves in the mirror are chimps and dolphins. They do this test where they put a blob of red on the chimp's nose, and when it looks in the mirror the chimp sees the blob and wipes it off. Other animals just think the thing in the mirror is another dog or whatever. So maybe in Tina's head she was as big as a wolf.

While I was thinking about how you can have a wrong idea about how strong you are and what you can take on, Kenny said, "This is rubbish. Can we go home now?"

"We've got to get to the next village to pick up the bus," I said. "We're probably nearly there."

Just as I spoke, the snow started to fall hard again. I looked at Kenny and noticed for the first time how cold he was. He was badly dressed for a walk like this, on the hills in a blizzard. Just a sweatshirt and a denim jacket and his jeans. And trainers that were already sodden. His nose was red and a line of thin snot dripped down, dabbed every few seconds with the back of his raw hand. He'd folded and hunched himself inside his jacket to try to keep out the cold, but it was like trying to get full up by eating soup.

I felt an idiot. It was my job to keep Kenny safe. I'd let him down. I should have thought ahead and planned for the worst. I unwrapped my scarf and yanked off the hat and gloves. Instantly the chill bit into me, like rats at cheese.

"Here," I said, "put these on and don't bloody moan about it."

Kenny used to act like having to wear warm clothes was some terrible punishment, like being made to eat his vegetables. But this time he stared at the bundle in my hands for a moment and then took it. He put the hat and gloves on, and I helped him with the scarf.

"I can do it!" he snapped, and pulled away.

Tina looked from one to the other of us, not knowing what was going on.

Then Kenny said, "Ta." And then, after another pause, "You'll be cold now."

I shrugged. "Nah," I told him. "But let's get moving. Can't be far to go."

Five

I was wrong. Another twenty minutes of trudging and we were still in the middle of nowhere. All along, the footpath had been skirting the edge of the higher hills. I wondered for a moment if we'd just been going around in circles.

"Hang on, Kenny," I said. "Let's see if we can't work this out from the map."

I took the map out of my pocket. My hands were so cold I dropped it in the snow. Kenny picked it up for me, his hands warm but clumsy in the gloves. I found the path on the map and followed it with my finger, trying to work out how far we'd come. Then I remembered my phone. It had Google Maps on it, which would tell us where we were.

But, of course, when I checked, there was no signal. I went back to the paper map and tried to guess where we were.

"Can we go back to where we got off the bus?" Kenny said.

"Dunno," I said. "Maybe. Yeah. At least we know the way."

But I hated the thought of retracing our steps. It would be like we'd given in, letting the stupid moors and the stupid snow beat us.

I looked again at the printed-out map. The path went in a big curve. The village we were heading for looked like it was exactly on the other side of the hill we were going around.

"I've got an idea, Kenny," I said.

"What?"

"Shortcut. Up and over." I pointed up the side of the hill and did a little whistle that went high then low. "What do you reckon?"

I thought Kenny would be all for it, but his face was strangely blank and his eyes were dull.

"Looks rotten up there," Kenny said. "And there int a path. What if we get lost?"

"We can't get lost. The path goes right round this hill. We go up, we go down – there's no way we could miss it. In fact, when we get to the top we should be able to see the village."

"All right," he said. "But quick. I'm dying of this cold."

To get up the side of the hill we first had to clamber over a stone wall. It was one of those walls that are made of stones just piled up on each other, with nothing sticking them together. Well, I say "just piled up", but you could see how cleverly they were stacked, with no spaces in between them.

"See, Kenny," I said. "It's like a stone jigsaw puzzle."

But Kenny wasn't in the mood to enjoy the craftsmanship.

It was easy enough to climb over the wall, apart from having Tina. I scrambled up first, then got Kenny to pass her to me. I jumped down and thought Tina would follow, but she just paced nervously along the top of the wall.

"Getting a bit old for this sort of lark, aren't you?" I said, and I picked Tina up and put her down in the snow on this side of the wall. The snow was deeper here, where the wind had blown it into drifts.

Kenny followed us, but as he jumped down he knocked one of the stones off the top. Kenny has always been a bit clumsy. He bent to pick it up.

"Just leave it," I said.

Kenny gave me a dirty look.

"Gotta fix it," he told me. "That's only fair."

The stone made a satisfying clunk as he laid it on top of the wall. Then he straightened it up, so it looked nice again.

"Don't be all day about it," I said.

I had a flashback to when we were young 'uns – Kenny five, me four, or something like that. It was before Mum left, and things were still OK at home. We had these wooden building blocks and a little wooden cart thing with red plastic wheels to push them around in. It was Kenny's favourite toy. He used to spend hours piling the bricks up. He always tried to make a tall skinny tower, with just one block on each level. But because he built it on the carpet, the tower would never get very high before it fell down. I was too young back then to understand that Kenny didn't always get things the way other kids did. I used to tell him to build it wider, with four blocks at the bottom, but he didn't like that.

"Want it high!" he'd yell. "Up. Up. Up."

Each time the tower fell, Kenny got more upset. He wanted to do it himself, but he just couldn't. So in the end I'd help him. I'd find a flat surface on the kitchen floor or on the tiles around the gas fire. And we'd take it in turns, one brick from him, one from me. And I'd make little adjustments so that it would stand.

And then, when all the blocks were used up, Kenny would lie down next to it and gaze up at the tower of wooden blocks. I don't know what he was thinking. Maybe imagining a tiny version of himself climbing up the tower and then standing at the top to look down over the world. After a while, he'd reach out and knock the tower down. The blocks would tumble over him, which always made him laugh. And it's true that the best thing about building a tower is knocking it down. But only when you've decided the time is right.

Six

It was much harder walking up the hill. My feet sank out of sight in the snow with each step. And under the snow and the grass, the mud was frozen solid into hard ruts. The uneven ground caught and tripped you or made you twist over on your ankle. And after a few minutes, the wind got up even higher and the snow blew around. It wasn't easy to tell what was coming down from the sky and what was blown up from the ground.

I looked ahead. We weren't far, now, from the top of the hill. Beyond it was just that endless grey nothing of the sky. I imagined the fields sloping down to the village beyond.

I turned and saw Kenny stumbling through the snow. "It's OK, Kenny," I said, almost shouting it. "We're nearly there."

Kenny looked up and half smiled. He walked a bit faster, dragging Tina along behind him. In five minutes we'd made it to the top of the hill.

Except it wasn't the top of the hill.

It was just a ridge. Beyond it the ground fell for a few metres and then climbed again.

My heart sank. But I had to hide my disappointment from Kenny.

"Sorry, Kenny," I said, putting on a bright voice. "False alarm. That's the top, over there. Downhill all the way after that. We'll have a cup of tea and some cake in the village."

"Sausage roll," Kenny said.

"Chips!" I added.

We ran down the short slope, trying to get some momentum for the climb. Tina enjoyed the little run, barking and scampering along in our tracks. But soon the three of us were trudging on up again. We had our heads low, as if we could duck the wind, the way the hero in a film ducks a sloppy punch from a drunk guy.

"Tell me more about what we'll have to eat," Kenny said when we were halfway up the next slope.

"What have we got so far?"

"Tea, cake, sausage rolls, chips."

"What else do you want?" I asked.

Kenny considered this for a few moments.

"More chips," he said.

"More chips it is, then. What else?"

"Another sausage roll."

"Coming right up," I promised.

"And then more cake."

"Same cake as the first one, or a different kind?"

"What was the first kind?" Kenny asked.

"Chocolate. With Smarties on top."

"OK, then," Kenny said. "For cake seconds I want more chocolate cake. And can I have the Smarties off of yours?"

"No way!" I said.

"Go on."

"Tell you what, you can have the Smarties from my second piece of cake, but I want the ones on the first. Deal?"

Kenny thought about it for a while, weighing it up. Finally, he nodded, as if making a big sacrifice, and said, "Deal."

He stuck out his hand and we shook on it.

Seven

About then I noticed that the solid grey of the sky had changed. At first I thought it was just that the clouds had got even thicker, but then I realised that it was getting late in the afternoon. Somewhere out beyond the clouds, the sun was going down.

Kenny was dragging his feet, going slower than a sloth with three legs walking in treacle. "Come on, Kenny," I said, "we don't want to be out at night with the gytrash on the prowl."

"The guy what?" he said, as I knew he would.

"Gytrash."

"What the bloody hell's a gytrash?" Kenny asked.

"They sometimes call it the shagfoal."

Kenny laughed nervously. "You're just making it up."

"Hah, it's true," I told him. "It's a special kind of Yorkshire monster that hangs out on the moors. Sometimes it looks like a big black dog, and sometimes it looks like a horse – but a horse with claws, not hooves. But whether it's in the shape of a horse or a dog, it always has red eyes, and that's how you know it. You see them glowing in the dark."

"What does it do to you?" Kenny asked.

"It leads you away from the right path."

"Then what?"

"No one knows," I said.

"How come?"

"Cos you're never seen again."

There was a pause as Kenny thought about it, then he said, "What does it do to you?"

"Eats you."

Kenny chewed that one over.

"If you're never seen again, how come you know it eats you?" Kenny asked.

"Because sometimes they find what's been left after it's finished eating you."

"Why, what's left?"

"Something and nothing," I said.

"How can it be something and nothing?"

"Just is."

"That doesn't make sense," Kenny complained.

"It does."

"So what is it, then?" Kenny asked. "The thing that's left?"

"Your bum hole!" I yelled.

Kenny barked out a laugh. "You mean the skin and, er, bits of bum?" he said.

"No, just the hole."

"How can that be? You mean just the air where it was? How would you find it?"

"Because it's your bum hole," I told him. "It's black and it smells."

And then I couldn't keep it up any more and I started laughing. Kenny joined in, and this time he managed to give me a good shove and I fell on my arse in a drift.

Eight

A bit later, Tina stopped dead and refused to budge. Kenny tried to pull her along, but she dug her feet in the snow.

"I think she's too tired to walk," Kenny said.

"Come here, then, girl," I said, and picked her up. She was shivering but felt warm against my freezing hands. She was only a little dog and no effort at all to carry.

We came to another wall. This one was higher than the first, and I wasn't sure I could climb over it while carrying Tina.

I looked along the length of it.

"There. There's a gate," I said.

We walked to the gate and scrambled over it. It seemed easier than scraping the gate open over the frozen ground.

We clumped down together on the far side, and then Kenny let out a scream of wild terror. He began to run at an angle across the field. At the same moment, I saw a flash of black fur, pointed claws and burning red eyes. The gytrash was upon us – I knew it, even though I'd thought it was just a stupid legend and that the gytrash didn't live anywhere apart from in old books. I dropped Tina, her barks and my screams joining with Kenny's. And I ran like a madman to catch up with him, Tina frantic at my ankles, the lead still attached to her collar and bouncing along after her.

Then I heard the unearthly sound of some wild thing and glanced behind me, still half expecting to see the slobbering gytrash bounding towards us.

Three or four black sheep bleated in alarm and skittered away from us along the line of the wall. Tina growled at them as they vanished into the whiteness. I thought she was going to chase them, so I grabbed her lead.

"Kenny, it's just sheep!" I cried out, my words breaking up into laughter. Kenny ran on a bit more, then stopped and turned, and I caught him up. We were both totally out of breath.

"Just. Sheep. Kenny," I panted.

"Yeah, I knew," he lied, and we both laughed again.

"Don't tell anyone we ran from the sheep," Kenny said.

"Not likely," I said. "I screamed louder than you did!"

Then we carried on, still heading towards the top of the hill. But my sense of where we were was all messed up somehow, just from that short mad run, along with the diversion down to the gate before it. And the greyness closed in until it felt like the sky was down here, all around us.

And then the snow came again, harder, so you could hear the sound of it tutting as it hit your jacket. We'd got a sweat on from our mad sprint from the gytrash, but that turned to a clammy chill on our backs. The three of us, with Tina back inside my jacket, were soon shivering.

"I h-hate it here," Kenny stuttered.

"We'll soon be out of it," I said, and I forced myself to grin at him. "Triple chips!"

"Don't want bloody chips!" Kenny snapped. "Want to go home. Want to go home NOW."

And then Kenny started running again, not from the gytrash but towards the promise of warmth and safety.

"Hold on, Kenny," I called out. "Stop it. I can't ... I've got Tina!"

I scrambled after him, but it was impossible to keep up. His long legs ate up the ground, and I kept stumbling because I couldn't put out my hands to balance.

"Wait, Kenny. Wait," I shouted again, but the snow and the cold grey sky swallowed my voice.

I ran on, ever higher, until my thigh muscles burned with the effort and my breath came in agonised gasps. I stopped and yelled again, or tried to, but I was knackered. All that came out was a croaky wheeze that turned into a hacking cough.

I put Tina down and then collapsed on my knees. I'd got another sweat on from the run, but, like before, the sweat soon turned as cold as death. I knew that Polar explorers fear sweat more than anything. It wets you from the inside out, and then your clothes don't keep out the cold, and you die. I climbed back to my feet and looked around.

"Kenny!" I screamed as loud as I could. Again, it was as if the sound couldn't get past the cold air and the blowing snow. It was like I was shouting into a pillow.

I started to panic. What if I couldn't find Kenny? What if he was lost on this stupid hill, wandering around? I looked at my watch. It was nearly four. It was growing darker all the time. Kenny, alone and lost, in the dark. I screamed again, "Kenny! Kenny!"

"No need to bloody shout."

It was Kenny. He was just there, right next to me. I grabbed him in a hug that was also meant to be a punishment.

"Kenny," I said. "If you eff off again like that, I'm having all your chips for the rest of your life."

Kenny looked down, but I don't think it was the chips.

"I thought if I started running I'd get there before I stopped. But I ran out of air."

Even after the hug was finished, we stood close to each other, our arms touching. In our family you don't say stuff like "I love you". You show it by standing like this, with your arms touching. Or by sitting together on the couch watching the telly, or by joking with each other while you're eating your cornflakes. Or by your dad putting his big rough hand in your hair and saying, "Come on, daft lad, let's get a pizza ordered." Tina stuck her nose out from my jacket and licked my face and then Kenny's. The lick was hot then cold, like the sweat on my back.

"Where are we, Nicky?" Kenny asked. "Where are we?"

I didn't want to say that I had no real idea. I got my phone out. No reception. Not a hint of a bar. Then I tried the printed-out map, unfolding it with my icy fingers. A few flakes of snow landed on it, and I brushed them away, leaving tracks of ink across the paper.

I saw the path we'd started out on – the path we should have stuck to.

"We're somewhere here," I said as I pointed at the blank space between the path and the village. It wasn't a contour map, where lines show you how steep the land is. There was nothing there. Or almost nothing …

"What's that?" Kenny said. He put a finger on a line that passed in between where I thought we must be and the top of the hill.

"Er, dunno," I said. "A path? No, wait, it's too wiggly. I think it's a little stream."

"Will there be fish?"

"Yeah, course. Bound to be."

Kenny was still pondering. "But it's in the way," he said.

"Yeah, but it's only a stream. We can jump it. And when we get past that, it'll be downhill all the way."

"Like Dad?" Kenny asked.

"Eh?"

"When Dad was at school. Them stories ... about the beck."

"Oh, yeah."

Funny how Kenny had remembered that. There was a beck – a narrow stream – just next to my dad's old school. Back in the olden days, when there were only three channels on the telly and the internet hadn't been invented, the best thing they used to do was jumping the beck after school.

I picked up Tina again, and we marched on through the drifting snow.

Nine

We came to the beck maybe fifteen minutes later.
I heard it before I saw it. It sounded like a football
crowd, or a forest.

"Nearly there, Kenny," I said.

Kenny looked up and said, "Good" and that was
all.

A few seconds later we reached it, and all the
hope and excitement drained out of me. It was
more like a river than a stream. Three or four
metres across.

"I can't jump that," Kenny said. "No way."

I peered at the stream, trying to work out if we
could wade across. There were small waterfalls –
just a few centimetres high, where the water was
white. And brown parts, the colour of tea, where
the stream moved slowly.

The trouble was that the slow parts looked quite deep. On a hot day it would have been fun to wade and splash across. But we were already cold to the bone. To be soaked through as well as cold ... I crouched and put my fingertips in the water. I thought my hands couldn't get any colder, but this was a different type of cold. It was a killing cold.

"It's no use, Kenny," I said. "We'll have to go around it."

I got the map out of my pocket again. It was so creased now that it was hard to read. And more melted snow had got onto it, smearing more of the ink. But I could still just make out the line of the stream. I guessed roughly where we must be, and followed the stream on the map. It went back until it joined the path we'd been on. And it looked like the path went over the stream, so there must be a bridge. I let my finger follow the stream further. Just near the edge of the printed page there was a main road and another, bigger, bridge. Yet here on this hillside, lost in the snow, it felt like we were completely cut off from the rest of the world. It was a bit weird to know there was a proper road out there, cutting into this wilderness.

If we followed the stream back to the path, we'd have wasted an hour of climbing up this bloody hill. But that couldn't be helped. Jenny used to say that sometimes you mess up. It's what you do next that counts. There's no mess so bad that it can't be cleared up. Something like that, anyway. Sometimes you have to go back so you can go forward.

I tried to show Kenny the way we had to go. But he was dulled by the cold, and his eyes were glazed. He just wanted out. I put my arm around him, but I had to stand on my tiptoes to do it, as he was much taller than me.

"At least it's downhill," I said.

"OK."

"And let's keep moving. It's freezing when you stop."

As we followed the stream, I realised with relief that we were on a sort of track. It wasn't like the real path, the one we'd left. It was more just that lots of people must have come this way before, so all the feet had made a trail.

For the first time, the walk was almost fun. The stream snaked back and forth as it ran down the side of the hill. There's something about walking along by the side of a stream or river that takes away your sadness and eases your fears. Rivers always go somewhere. Rivers never get lost. Follow it, and you'll be OK.

Kenny's tread became less tired, and he got a bit more of the old bounce back in his stride. Even the snow seemed to ease off. But then I realised that it was just because we'd turned away from the wind, so the snow blew into our backs rather than our faces. And even the snowy wind at our backs felt like a good thing – a force helping us to get where we wanted. I put Tina down for a minute, but she whined and whimpered till I picked her up and slipped her back inside my jacket.

"Tell us a story," Kenny said. "Not a scary one."

I'd always told stories to Kenny. Sometimes I read them from books, sometimes I made them up. I think he liked the ones I made up more than the ones from books, because the made-up ones often had places and people he knew in them.

"What kind of story, our Kenny?" I asked.

"A good one."

"Daft lad! All my stories are good."

"One with adventures in it," Kenny said.

Adventures. That was tricky. I tried to think of some of the stories I'd read. Old ones, mainly ...

"I'm waiting ..." Kenny reminded me.

So I told Kenny all the stories I could think of. Stories about the Greeks fighting the Trojans, all because of some girl everyone fancied.

"What was she called, the girl?" Kenny asked.

"Eh, oh, Helen, I think," I said.

"Helen? That's not an olden-days name. There's a Helen in my class. She's got metal on her teeth to make them straight. She was kissing a boy in the playground and they got stuck together, because he had metal teeth as well. They had to get the fire brigade to chop them into two again."

"No way!" I said.

"They did!" Kenny told me. "Well, I wasn't there, but that's what I heard. They would have been stuck together for ever. They would have had to get married and live like that."

"How would they eat if their mouths were stuck together?"

"I don't know. Doctors would put a pipe in them to pour soup down."

"A pipe? Where would they put it?" I asked.

"I don't know. Up the bum probably."

Kenny said this in a matter-of-fact way, but that just made it more funny, and it was ages before I could finish the story, about how the Greeks only won because they hid inside a giant wooden horse, and the Trojans dragged the horse inside the city. And then the Greeks sneaked out in the night and burned the city down. They killed nearly all the Trojans and took back Helen.

"What did they take the horse into their city for?" said Kenny. "That were stupid. They should have looked inside it. They should have set it on fire."

And I didn't really have an answer for that.

Next I told Kenny about King Arthur and his knights, and how they spent all their time fighting each other and rescuing ladies from castles. I said how loads of them died looking for some cup full of Jesus's blood. And at the end there was a great battle, and Arthur's son was in charge of the baddies, and Arthur killed him but got a mortal wound himself. I told him that Arthur went off to die on an island, but he might not have, and he might be coming back with all his men when we need him most, shining like gold.

Ten

As we'd walked our way through the stories, the
landscape changed. It was almost as if the world
was changing to fit in with the stories. First a few
bushes and tiny tree saplings began to line the
banks of the stream. Then the banks on both sides
rose up, so that the stream was below us – except
it was even more like a river now. Then trees grew
around and over us, and that was good because
we were more sheltered from the snow and the
wind. The trees were mainly bare, but if you looked
closely you could see buds beginning to emerge –
tight fists of life waiting to open out into a green
hand.

Not so good was the fact it was getting dark.
We hadn't seen the sun all day, just rainy greyness
turning into snowy greyness. So it wasn't as if

you could see the sun sinking, or even sense it. It was just like one of those dimmer switches, with someone gradually turning the lights down.

"Why aren't we there yet?" Kenny asked.

"Won't be long. The river will cross the path in a few minutes, and before you know it, it'll be chip-butty time."

Just then the bank we were on took a turn upwards, and the stream fell even further below. The sound of the water deepened into a roar, and big rocks barged out from the surface. There were no still parts of the river, and everything was white. We walked on. I looked across at the other bank and saw that the stream had carved a canyon, and the walls were shining rock.

The drop down to the water now was almost as tall as the side of a house. It would have been dangerous, but someone had put up a wooden fence to stop you falling over the edge.

The snow had stopped, or rather turned back to wet sleet. And the trees were thicker here, so that there wasn't much snow lying on the ground. I took Tina out of my jacket and put her down. She looked happy to be among the trees and cocked her leg a few times.

I was suddenly starving. And then I
remembered that we didn't have to find the village
to have something to eat.

"Kenny," I said. "The sarnies!"

"What?" Kenny asked. "Oh yeah! And there's
pop left."

Kenny was carrying the bag on his back. It
had been there in plain sight all along. We stood
next to the fence, looking down on the stream.
It was frothing and raging below, but it seemed
more happy than angry. It reminded me of being
at junior school when the bell for the end of the
day went. You sprinted out of the school gates,
screaming and leaping for joy.

Kenny dug down into the Adidas bag. He'd put
the sandwiches back inside the empty bag from the
sliced bread and then tied a knot in the neck. He
had to take my gloves off to untie it. For a second
I thought how nice and snug it must have been for
his fingers wrapped up in the warm wool.

"What shall I have first – cheese or jam?" I said.
Already my mouth was filling up with saliva.

"Eh?" Kenny asked, as if I'd said something in
Chinese.

"Oh, never mind. Just give me whatever comes
out."

Kenny reached down inside the plastic bag and pulled out a sandwich. I grabbed it and took a massive bite.

I nearly puked. I spat out what I'd bitten. Then I grabbed the cola bottle and had a good swig.

"Shit, Kenny, what the bloody hell is that?" I said.

Kenny looked at me, still clearly puzzled. "Sandwich ..."

"Yeah, but what ...?"

"Cheese and jam," Kenny told me. "Like you said."

"You put cheese and jam in the same sandwich?"

"Yeah. You said to."

"I told you to make cheese sandwiches and jam sandwiches," I said.

"You said cheese and jam. So that's what I done."

Then Kenny took one of the sandwiches and started to eat it. He chewed it slowly for a while, as if he was considering some deep problem about the meaning of life.

"Tastes all right," Kenny said.

"Nutter," I said, and I tried not to smile. Then I had another bite of my sandwich.

"I've had worse things for dinner," I said.

I was remembering some of the things that Dad used to try to cook when he was still on the booze and not coping, back in the days before Jenny came and sorted him out. One time one of his mates gave him a pheasant he'd run over in his van. He said that he'd hung the pheasant and that it was ready. My dad had been on a bender for a few days and didn't know what to do with it. He just put the whole thing in the oven – feet, feathers, guts and all.

It was a beautiful bird, despite being a bit squashed from getting run over by the van. I remembered the shimmering greeny-blue of its head and the vivid blood-red of the patch around the yellow eye. Even the golden-brown of its back was beautiful when you looked at it – millions of different shades from yellow to black and everything in between. And then the two long, proud tail feathers, with stripes like a railway line going to heaven. Anyway, Dad put it in the oven and then fell asleep on the couch. Me and Kenny were starving. All we'd had to eat for a few days was toast. Not even toast with butter or marge – just toast.

So me and Kenny waited, somehow thinking it would come out like a roast chicken you'd see on the telly. We probably weren't seeing things straight because of the hunger. We used to itch a lot, too, back in those days. And I don't think we smelled that great ...

Talking of which, it was the smell that got to us first. It was rank. Mainly the feathers burning, I guess. Mixed in with the bird shit left in the pheasant's guts, cos it hadn't been cleaned, like I said ... But because we were there all the time and the smell came on gradually, we didn't really notice it.

We had no idea how long to cook it for. All I can remember is us sitting in the kitchen waiting for it to be ready.

And then there was a muffled bang from the oven, like someone dropping a heavy bag. I opened the oven door and black smoke spilled out. And there was a stench like a tramp had shat himself and then set his underpants on fire.

I turned the oven off, and me and Kenny ran out into the garden before the stink and smoke killed us. Ten minutes later, we came back. My dad was still out of it on the couch, but he mumbled and coughed in his sleep.

I took the pheasant out of the oven. If I hadn't seen my dad put it in, I'd never have guessed what it was. It looked like some terrible experiment that had gone wrong. Blackened feathers, bits of inside, bits of outside.

"I think it blowed up," Kenny said.

We had toast again for dinner.

I took another bite of the cheese and jam sandwich Kenny had made. Now I was expecting it, the taste wasn't so bad. I made myself imagine it was pickle, not jam. Anyway, I was starving hungry and freezing cold, and the sandwich helped.

I stood by the fence and looked down at the gorge. The cliffs on each side, the rocks sticking up from the stream and the rapids made it look like something you'd see on a documentary about the wilds of America or Russia or somewhere. Just a bit smaller. You could almost imagine bears hunting for salmon in the river and wolves prowling among the trees.

"I like it here," Kenny said.

"Yeah, it's not bad, is it? And it won't be long now till we hit that path. Then we'll find the road and the village, and it'll all be sound. But let's see if there's a signal on this stupid phone, and I'll tell Dad that we'll be home a bit late."

I reached for the phone in my jacket pocket. My hands were so cold they were as clumsy as flippers. Still no signal, and the battery was down to almost nothing. I held it high, which was stupid – as if an extra six inches would make a difference when the signal has to come all the way down from a satellite that's orbiting the Earth thousands of kilometres away. Maybe a bit less stupidly I leaned out a little bit, over the fence, then over the cliff and over the water, thinking that maybe that would help.

And then, for no good reason, the phone fell out of my hand. One second I was holding it, the next second I wasn't. I saw it slip from my fingers and begin to tumble, turning slowly in the air. I didn't have time to think much then, not proper stretched-out thoughts. But maybe a few images flashed into my mind. Jenny, nice Jenny. She'd saved my dad, and so saved us. She'd given me the phone, paid for out of her hard-earned money from working night shifts as a nurse.

And so I lunged out after the falling phone. I felt the top of the fence press against my thighs, holding me steady. I stretched a bit further and my fingers just reached the phone. But I couldn't catch it cleanly. The phone flipped up, and I knew I had it. Like when you go to catch a cricket ball and it bounces out of your hands but pops up and you know you can get it with the second grab.

And I did. I got the phone. But leaning out that extra few centimetres was too much for the rotten wood of the fence. I heard the crack and felt the fence give. I half turned so that I could see Kenny. I saw his mouth changing shape – from a wide smile to an "o" of horror.

And then I was falling.

Eleven

I think that half turn before I fell saved my life. Without it, I'd have gone straight down – head first onto the rocks beneath. Would you die if you fell down seven or eight metres? Maybe I'd just have broken my neck and spent the rest of my life in a wheelchair, only being able to communicate by blinking.

Anyway, that half turn meant I was able to throw out my arm, and I just managed to catch the edge of the cliff. There was no way I was ever going to stop myself from falling, but my desperate grab at the cliff slowed my fall. It made sure that I slithered down feet fist, crashing and bashing into the rocky cliff face as I went. My head took one big smash on a jutting fist of rock, but I hit the bottom before I registered it, and then there was a different kind of pain.

It's a funny thing, pain. When it happens, it's the most important thing in the world – a stubbed toe, a burned finger, a bad tooth. You live inside the pain. The pain becomes you. If it's bad enough, you'd do anything to make it stop. You'd even betray your friend (or your brother). And then it goes away and you forget it. It's as if you never had the pain. It must be because it's impossible to remember pain the way you remember other things. Like a times table at school, or the French for dog, or where you put your secret stash of sweets. That kind of remembering means bringing the things back into your head. But to remember a pain would mean having the pain again, same as before, and that's not how it is. So all you can remember is how you felt about the pain, but not the pain itself. And even that comes back in a weak way, like orange squash with too much water in it. There isn't the horror you had the first time round.

So now, when I talk about this, it's just words – words that I've tried to make true. But they'll never take me back – back to landing on the broken rocks by the side of the stream.

Instead of me feeling the hardness of the fall, I felt a weird softness. I expected an awful jolt as my legs hit, but it was as if I'd landed in sand. In fact, for a second I thought that's just what had happened – that I'd been lucky and picked out some patch of sand or mud to land in.

Except that I slumped forwards and realised that there was only rock. And that the feeling in my legs was changing. The soft feeling was mixed now with something dark and terrible. It was the sort of feeling you get when you're being chased in a dream by some faceless monster. But the feeling wasn't fear in my head but fear in my legs. Yeah, that was it. The pain – a sick, grinding ache – began to grow like fear. A terror in my actual flesh and bones.

I heard a noise above the roar of the monster, the monster that was the stream.

Tina barking. And a voice. "Nicky! Nicky!"

And somehow I managed to shout back, "I'm all right, Kenny, I'm OK."

But I wasn't. I'd landed on a narrow section of flat rock and gravel in between the cliff and the rushing water of the stream. My hands were stinging – I'd come down feet first but then slapped down hard. I looked at my hands. It was only then that I realised the phone was gone. Dropped in the river or smashed on the rocks, I didn't know. One of my fingers was bent at a weird angle. It hurt, but I knew that wasn't the real problem.

I looked down at my legs, terrified about what I might see. I was on my side with my right leg on top of the left. I flexed my ankle and a jolt of white agony shot like a pinball up through my foot and my leg, right up into my head. I made a sound in between a groan and a scream.

"Nicky!" Kenny's voice came again. "Nicky!"

I thought about my brother up there on his own, not knowing.

"Just wait, Kenny," I gasped out, trying to make my voice carry to him. "Just give me a second."

My right ankle was screwed – that much I knew. But something worse had happened to my left leg, the one underneath. I didn't even try to move it. The sick feeling came from there. I had a picture in my mind. The kind of broken leg where the bones shatter and the ragged shards of it jab out from your skin.

I thought I was going to be sick.

But then I thought that there would be blood. Lots of blood. And my trousers didn't look bloody.

So it wasn't the sort of broken leg with bones poking out. I tried to reach down to touch it, but then another wave of pain came. Not the piercing white icy pain from my ankle but the slow surging fear that pulsed up from the other leg. And it wasn't that it hurt to move it. I couldn't. I didn't know if it was because I was paralysed, or if it was just some deep knowledge I had. A knowledge hidden in the bones themselves, which said "DO NOT MOVE".

More yapping from Tina. I tried to twist myself so I could look up, catch Kenny's eye.

But it was darker now. The sky was the colour of the painting water you dip your brushes in at school, the colours all running together to make a swirl of purple-black.

"Kenny, I'm all right," I said. "I'm fine. I just need you to do something. I need you to carry on by the stream until you get to the road. And then you've got to stop a car and tell them what's happened. Tell them I've fallen down and I need help. They'll know what to do."

Well, that's sort of what I said. It might not have made as much sense, and there was a bit of gasping and groaning mixed in with it, but that was the gist.

It was wasted. There was more frantic barking from Tina, and then I saw something darker moving against the shadows of the cliff.

"Kenny!" I yelled. "Get back! Don't be an idiot!"

He was trying to climb down. He was a good climber, Kenny. No tree he couldn't get up. But this was wet rock. Two of us in a heap at the bottom would be seriously bad news.

But Kenny was doing OK. There were hand holds and foot holds in the rock. There were stubby shrubs and bushes growing out of it. Kenny was halfway down, then two thirds down, when one of the bushes sticking out betrayed him. I saw him pull away from the rock face and fall towards me. I thought he was going to land right on me. I thought about the agony that would be to my legs more than I thought about Kenny.

But the climb had taken him a little away from me. He landed with a grunt on his feet and then fell back on his arse.

"Jesus, Kenny, are you OK?" I said.

Kenny sat up and turned to me. He looked sort of funny in his Leeds United hat and scarf.

"Yeah," Kenny said. "Sore bum. I thought you were ... I thought you were badly ..."

"I'm all right, Ken," I said. And then, after a second, I added, "Except my leg. It's broken, I think. Hurts like buggery."

I mostly kept bad things from Kenny, but that was when I thought there was no point making him worried or sad. Now I had to let him know that we were in trouble.

And then I heard Tina barking again. She was still at the top of the cliff, going frantic. And then the barking stopped and I heard her small feet scrabbling at the cliff.

"Kenny," I said. "I think Tina's going to—"

But she already had. Somehow, she had found a way down, with no more fuss than if she'd just run down the stairs at home.

She came up to my face and sniffed, and then went to my legs and sniffed again. And then she came beside me, turned around and lay down, her body warm against me.

Twelve

So there we were, the three of us, by the side of the stream that had turned into a river, raging with white water, in the near dark, in the middle of absolutely nowhere. And I hurt so much I thought I was going to vomit.

"You look … not good," Kenny said.

"Why did you come down, Kenny?" I groaned after a couple of seconds – seconds I spent trying not to scream.

"I couldn't leave you here on your own," Kenny replied. "What would Dad say?"

I was still lying twisted on the rocks. I managed to sit up, but the pain made me whine and whimper like a whipped dog. It was even darker down here, almost full-night, so I could hardly see Kenny.

"Kenny, you need to go and get help," I finally gasped.

"No! *I'll* help you. We can … I'll carry you! It'll be a piece of piss. Dad says he's done farts that weigh more than you do."

That made me laugh – I remembered Dad saying it when he swung me round as a kid. I couldn't believe that Kenny remembered it, too. It's funny what stuck in his head. But my laugh turned into a spluttering cough as the pain surged and raged again.

"You can't carry me, Kenny. I'm bigger now, and my legs hurt too much. You've got to climb back up there. Can you do it?"

Kenny looked back up the side of the gorge. "I can try, but it's very slidy," he said. "You can slide down, but you can't slide up."

"Have a go," I said. "You've got to be like Spiderman. But be careful. Then get to the road, fast as you can, and wave down a car. It's the countryside. People are nice. They'll stop. Tell them what's happened. Tell them they need to call for help. Police and ambulance."

"But I don't want to leave you by yourself."

"I've got Tina for company."

"It's nearly night time," Kenny said. I don't know if he was thinking about me here by the river or him being chased by the gytrash with its red eyes.

"Just stay by the river. It'll take you straight to the road. And, Kenny ..."

"Yeah?"

"You've got to go now. I'm hurt ... my legs are all ruined."

Normally, Kenny didn't do hugs any more. When we were younger, he would hug anyone. But someone at his school must have told him hugging was for babies, so he stopped. But he knelt down next to me now and tried to give me an awkward hug. I kissed the top of his head. I don't know why.

And then Kenny began to climb back up the side of the gorge. It looked easy at first, because there were broken rocks for him to scramble up. And then he slowed, and I heard his grunts of effort. Dirt and pebbles skittered down.

"Careful, Kenny," I shouted, and the shout hurt like fire.

I saw Kenny leaning backwards in the gloom, and I guessed the rock must overhang there. I saw his legs kicking at nothing, moving in mid-air. And then he fell back again. It was only two or three metres up, not even halfway to the top, but he grunted with pain when he landed.

"Kenny, Kenny, you OK?"

"Yeah," he said, and got straight back up. "Try again."

This time he slithered down before he even reached the overhang.

He didn't pause, but tried once more, inching his way up. He made it to the overhang, but it was no good – only a professional climber could have got past it. Kenny was stuck, and I felt nothing but relief when he managed to scramble down again.

"Can't do it, our Nicky," Kenny said, no emotion in his voice.

I tried to get my head straight so I could think properly. But it was hard. My mind was all over the shop. Drifting forwards and backwards. And then I saw Kenny looking at me, calmly waiting for me to think of something.

Right, focus.

He could go back along the stream, to where the banks were less deep and easier to climb up. But back that way the river went right up to the rock walls of the gorge, without any flat bank. Kenny would have to wade in the icy water, and I didn't know how long for. We were both already frozen to the bone. Getting soaked might … Well, I didn't want to think about it.

The other way, downstream towards the road, looked easier. The water flowed even faster, but there was a dry bit of bank in between the stream and the wall of the gorge, and rocks you could scramble over. If that carried on for a while, there was a chance Kenny might make it to a place where he could climb up.

The shock of the fall had made me forget how freezing cold I was, but now the chattering of my teeth reminded me. It was like when we were kids and I used to make the sound of a machine gun. It was hard to speak. But I got the words out.

"That way, Kenny," I said. "Follow the stream that way, until you can climb up. The road can't be far. You can almost hear it."

And I did think that if I tried really hard I could pick out the sound of cars roaring somewhere in the distance. It was probably just the water thundering down the gorge, and the pain and the cold playing tricks with my head.

Kenny hesitated.

"I'm scared," he said.

"Don't be daft. I was just joking about the gytrash. It doesn't exist."

"Not of the monster."

"What then?" I asked Kenny. "That you'll get lost?"

"No."

"What?" That word came out more like w-w-w-t-t-t because of the chattering.

"I'm scared you might ... you might ..." Kenny started saying but couldn't finish. Then he hugged me again, and I felt his hot tears wet on my cold face.

"I'll be fine, our Kenny," I told him. "But you've got to move yourself."

"I don't want to be on my own."

"You'll never be on your own, Kenny. We'll always be together. But to be together, you've got to leave me now. Please. Please."

And then Kenny got up and walked away. Tina stood, too. She looked at Kenny and then looked at me. It really seemed like she was trying to work out who needed her more, but it was probably just her trying to decide what her best chance of surviving was. Anyway, Tina made her mind up and trotted off after Kenny. In a few seconds they had gone round a bend and I couldn't see them any more.

I was about to let out a huge scream of agony and fear, the scream I'd been holding in ever since I fell. Then Kenny came running back.

"Here," he said. "You need these." He took the scarf and the gloves off.

"No, Kenny, you have them. I bloody hate Leeds United."

"Put 'em on anyway," Kenny said. "I won't tell anyone."

I think he'd forgotten he was wearing the hat, or he'd have given me that, too. I didn't remind him. He wrapped the scarf around me and even stretched the gloves out while I slid my hands inside. The gloves were wet from his attempt to climb out, but they still felt good.

"I'll be back in two shakes of a lamb's tail," Kenny said, which was something my dad used to say when he was off out to the pub.

And then he was gone, and Tina with him.

Thirteen

I lay back down on the cold wet rock. I was
shivering and sick and frightened. If I stayed
completely still, the pain from my leg was only a
dull throb. But the tiniest movement was agony.
And now I was so alone.

How long would it be? If Kenny could find a
way back up onto the rough path by the stream
and then get to the road ... Well, twenty minutes?
Half an hour? But then he had to stop a car. What
if there weren't any? Who would be driving on the
moors at night? No, someone would. This wasn't
Outer Mongolia, it was bloody Yorkshire. People
everywhere. There hadn't been a single day of my
life that I hadn't seen people. That was the world.
It was full of people. You couldn't hide from them
if you wanted. You'd go into Leeds and there'd be

thousands, millions, billions of them, more than you could count. All swarming around, all different but all the same, and none of them knowing who you are. Even the village was getting like that. New houses, new people – people whose stories you'd never find out.

Cold.

And it was snowing again. The wind didn't reach down in the gorge, and the overhanging trees kept some of the snow off. But now it was snowing so hard that big wet flakes still reached me. One landed on my lips and I licked it off. It was nice. I hadn't realised how thirsty I was. I opened my mouth and hoped more flakes would drop in. But it's one of those things you learn as a kid: you can't drink rain or snow, no matter how hard it falls – even when it seems that the sky has more water in it than air.

I took a glove off and ran my hand over my wet hair, trying to scoop the snow off it. Then I licked my fingers. It was useless.

I tried to scrunch myself up, hiding from the snow. I needed to keep whatever warmth I had left wrapped up inside me. But my leg hurt too much to bend it. It was about then that I first thought I might really die there, freezing to death in the wet snow before Kenny found someone and brought them back to me.

That's when I started to yell. I suppose it was stupid for us not to have done it earlier. Another walker might have been on the path by the stream. But now I think I did it more as a cry of fear and rage at what was happening. I began by screaming "HELP! HELP!" but soon the words changed into a raw sound, an animal screech. I poured not just the pain and fear of now into my yells, but all the bad things that had happened in my life. My mum leaving us, my dad falling apart, me having to look after Kenny. The days I went to school hungry – properly hungry – because I gave Kenny the one slice of bread we had left. The days I went to school dirty because there was no hot water, and no one would sit next to me. The days when other kids at school made fun of me because my trousers were halfway up my legs.

And I screamed because Sarah didn't want to go out with me any more.

Sarah was my first ever girlfriend. I'd never kissed anyone before her. Never even touched another girl. Sarah was dark and pretty and clever, and she said five funny things for every one funny thing I could think of. She shouldn't ever really have gone out with me in the first place. It was all mixed up with her brother, who was my mortal enemy. But even he turned out to be all right in the end. And me and Sarah had three months together, and they were the best three months of my life. Everything was OK. My dad was good – mainly because of Jenny, who put all the things back in our lives that we'd been missing. Even Kenny was finding his way in the world. He loved his special school and the mates he had there. So what if his best friend thought he was Dr Who?

And then there was my mum. It was only last year that we found out what had happened to her and where she'd gone. She flipped when me and Kenny were small. Kenny was a lot to handle. So was our dad. Maybe so was I. Mum got depressed, went a bit mad. Left. For years we thought she didn't love us, didn't even think about us. Now we knew that she had a new life in Canada, but she'd never forgotten us. She'd invited us to go there and stay for the holidays, but we didn't have the money for that, so she was coming to us. I was still angry with Mum. Still filled up with feelings that no one could put a name to. But one of those feelings was love. So for the first time ever my life wasn't shit.

And then ...

And then Sarah told me that she just wanted to be friends. We were in Starbucks, where we'd had our first ever date.

"I think you're really nice," Sarah said. I knew straight away that everything was wrong. She said some other things, but the blood was beating in my ears and I couldn't take it in. My hands were on the table, balled up into fists. I remember her putting her hand on top of mine. The feel of it – cool and dry. And her perfect nails, not like my bitten stumps.

"What did I do?" I said, or something like that. Meaning, *What did I do wrong?*

"Nothing," Sarah said.

"Then why?"

"There's not always a good reason why. Sometimes it just is."

I couldn't look at her. I stared at my fists. She took her hand off them. In the three months we'd been going out, I'd got better at talking about my feelings. But now that was all over.

"I hate you," I said.

"No you don't," Sarah said.

Then no one said anything for a while, and when I looked up, she was gone.

Fourteen

Could I have fallen asleep down here? No, not quite
asleep. But in a weird trance – remembering and
thinking. Not properly asleep. It was too cold to
sleep.

I'd been lying on a slab of rock a few
centimetres above the level of the stream and back
from it, out of the spray. But something looked
different now. Felt different. Sounded different.
The water was closer. No, not just closer. I was in
it. Almost.

I didn't understand. In my daze, had I rolled
towards the water? No, that wasn't it. I hadn't
moved. Couldn't move. The river had. It was
growing. All this rain and snow. And here in the
gorge, the river had nowhere to go but up. I tried
to drag myself back from the edge. There was still

half a metre of dry stone under the cliff. Getting there hurt so much I screamed again, higher than last time. The scream rasped at my throat with its claws. It felt as if someone was pulling a great bramble bush out of me.

And now I felt a whole new type of fear. The water was going to continue to rise in the gorge. I couldn't escape, not with my messed-up legs. The river was going to creep up and take me in its cold arms and pull me into its black guts.

I'd had a terror of drowning ever since I was small. I don't know what set it off. Maybe I got out of my depth at the swimming pool. Maybe Dad had got drunk when I was a baby and dropped me in the bath. Whatever it was, it was a memory too bad to bring back. I used to imagine how drowning would feel – the panic as you take in your first lungful of water, trying to scream and call for help.

But then I read something in the library about drowning. It said that the way we imagine a drowning never really happens. The person doesn't splash and cry out and go down and then up and then down and up a few more times. It's silent, calm. You take in a lungful of water, and then that's it. Down you go, no struggling, nothing.

Smooth. And that made me even more scared of it, not less.

But I was being stupid and letting my thoughts get muddy with panic. Kenny would be at the road by now. Help was on its way. What would it be? A helicopter? I hoped it would be a helicopter. They'd send down a man with a stretcher and they'd winch me up. I'd be able to see the river, the gorge, the whole mountain, Yorkshire, England, the world, as I spun slowly round. A great story to tell everyone. I'd tell my dad, and Sarah, and then my mum. Everyone at school. I'd be famous. There'd be a special assembly. The head teacher would go on about what a hero I was. I'd go up on the stage in the hall, looking shy and embarrassed while everyone clapped and cheered. "Modest, isn't he?" I'd hear someone say. I'd get a medal. What was that one they gave you for bravery when you weren't in the army? The George Cross, that was it. Stupid name. Who's called George these days? It must have been after some king. And what brave things did kings ever do? Well, maybe they were brave in the olden days, riding into battle. But not now. How is it brave to sit in a palace or to go and open a new leisure centre? They have someone to put the toothpaste on their toothbrush, my dad

said. Someone to wipe their arse for them. Maybe
they might slice a finger off when they were cutting
a ribbon. Or get an ankle bitten by a corgi. A
yapping corgi. Yap, yap, yap.

Yapping.

I opened my eyes.

Fifteen

The water was even closer, and the roar of it was louder than ever. The stream really had changed into a raging torrent now. But that wasn't what I'd heard.

Barking.

Tina.

She was there. Here, I mean. Tina was trying to shake off the wet. Or was she shivering?

For a second I thought it meant that the rescuers were coming. Not winching down from a helicopter but doing the sensible thing and walking along the river. Maybe Kenny would be with them. I shouted out, "Hey! Here! Kenny!"

But it didn't feel ... right. There'd have been noise. Lights – yeah, they'd have torches. And why would they send Tina ahead of them?

No, this was something else. Something bad. Tina was here because something had gone wrong. I shouldn't have sent Kenny off on his own. I didn't know what lay past the bend in the river. It could be anything. A waterfall. Proper rapids. Or just a big flat area of water, reaching from wall to wall of the gorge.

I had to go and help. Had to get to Kenny.

But my bloody stupid useless legs.

Tina came close to me. She was whimpering and shivering. She scrunched herself next to me, trying to get warm.

"What's happened, girl?" I said. "What's happened?"

I wanted to lie here under the shelter of the rock. Lie and wait for the rescuers to come.

But they weren't coming. Kenny needed me. I had to be the rescuer.

My leg. I remembered something from the telly, where a guy got dropped in the jungle and told you how to survive. One of those programmes where they act like they're alone, even if they've got a massive film crew with them. And they go off every night to stay in a Premier Inn and eat at Nando's. Nando's ... Wish I hadn't thought of that. It's warm in Nando's. Food ...

Stop it, Nicky. Come back. Focus.

On the programme there was a thing about fixing a broken leg. Something about a splint. But then, if you didn't have a splint, something else you could do. What was it? Yes, tie one leg to the other one. Use the other leg as the splint. With your belt. Yes, that was the way.

I unbuckled my belt and slid it out from the loops. Even that small movement hurt like hell. I was afraid to touch the messed-up leg, but I knew I had to do something so I could move. I felt down along my left leg carefully to find out where the break was. Everything above my knee was OK. I prodded at my knee. Sore, but that wasn't the problem. I stretched and felt along the outside of my leg. Ten centimetres below my knee I came to it. A bulge, like an egg. Just touching it lightly wasn't too bad. My leg didn't seem to mind that. And, yeah, I know it's stupid, but I was coming to think of my leg as something different from me – a separate being. Separate, but the same. The black sheep of the family. Something to be embarrassed about. The leg definitely had a brain. Or at least a mind. It thought things and felt things. It had views and opinions. And the leg's main opinion was that it didn't want me to move it.

I knew the next bit was going to hurt. Hurt a lot. But now I wasn't just doing it for me. Kenny needed me. He was up ahead somewhere, stuck and in trouble.

I began to wrap the belt around my legs. The belt was an old one of my dad's and way too long. I remembered him poking extra holes in it with one of the tools from his toolbox. Looked like a screwdriver but with a sharp point on the end, not a flat bit. What did he call it? An owl? No, an awl. My dad was good with tools. Told me my granddad was even better. He was an engineer in the mine. He kept the machinery turning. And my granddad had passed his knowledge down to my dad. But bits of it had been lost. Forgotten. And my dad had tried to show me things. How to measure and mark the wood before you start to drill. How screws were better than nails. How to keep your chisel sharp. But I never really listened. What would I have to pass on to my kids, if I ever had any? Changing a sodding lightbulb freaked me out.

But these thoughts were all instead of the thing I was dreading. The thing I was putting off.

Kenny. Kenny. Kenny.

I reached the place where the egg grew from my leg. I lightly wrapped the belt around that, and then down as far as my ankle. My legs were now loosely tied together. But that was no good. I held my breath and tightened the belt. My scream filled the gorge, drowned the river, reached the sky, stretched out into space.

But even as I screamed, I carried on tightening the belt to bind my two legs together.

There was a weird taste in my mouth. I spat. Blood. What had I bitten? Tongue? Cheek? Or had the blood somehow come up from inside me?

It didn't matter now. The searing agony passed. I still had the loose end of the belt in my hand. The buckle end was clamped between my knees. I didn't know what to do with the loose end. It wouldn't reach back down to the buckle. I tucked it under and round one of the loops, and pulled it into a knot, as tightly as I could. More agony. But oddly, there was something "right" about this agony. The pain seemed to be saying, "Yes, this is the right thing to do," like the last stab of pain when you pull out a splinter.

I knotted the buckle end in the same way. Now my legs were tied tightly together. It felt ... better. Terrible, but better.

But the water was still rising. I felt the spray on my face. I glanced at Tina. She was shaking and looking as rotten as I felt.

"Come on, girl," I said, "walkies." I'd have laughed at my own stupid joke if I'd had the breath.

I began to crawl on my belly, like some stranded fish. Yeah, like an illustration I remembered seeing in a book about evolution. It was the first fish to pull itself out of the water, on its way to becoming an amphibian. That was evolution going forwards, but I felt I was going back, becoming that dull-eyed, cold-blooded animal. All that counted was crawling forward. The pain was nothing. I had to find Kenny.

Tina limped by my side, her head low, still shivering and trembling. Like she was an omen of something terrible.

Sixteen

I followed the way Kenny had gone, along the
broken rock and gravel by the side of the raging
stream. It was properly dark now, and the snow
was falling again. My ears were full of the roar
of the water. Sometimes Tina was at my ear,
sometimes she lagged behind.

The river curved to the left, and I followed it
round, digging my gloved fingers into the gravel
to drag myself forwards. The river grew wider
and the bank narrower with each metre. And then
there was no bank at all, and I was dragging myself
through shallow water.

I was moving slowly, so slowly, but I still jarred
my leg a couple of times on juts of rock. It was like
I'd been hit with an iron bar, and I bellowed out my
pain and rage and frustration.

And then it was as if the volume knob on the river had been turned up all the way. I saw that I'd come to a waterfall. The water only fell a metre or so, but I was so close it sounded like all the toilets in the world flushing together. The bank took two steep steps down, and this was the worst part of the awful journey.

I mean the worst in terms of physical pain.

The real worst part was yet to come.

I knew the steps were going to hurt. I bent my legs to try to keep the broken bone away from the rock, and I slithered down. The rock pulled up my jacket and jumper and shirt. It cut into my guts, scraping the skin off, and my face crunched into the slimy gravel at the bottom. But on I went.

I don't know how long it took me to drag myself around the bend in the river. But once I'd made it, filthy and cold and drenched, I wished I hadn't.

The river was different here.

It didn't surge and froth and shake its white fists at the sky. The river was gentle and slow. The snowflakes fell on its surface and floated for a while like tears on a face. It was the size of a big room, and the still water stretched out to the next bend in the river. I could hear another waterfall, out of my sight. This was just a calm section in between the rapids.

The cliffs on each side were lower here – not the height of a house, but a bungalow. The water lapped right to the edge on each side. There was no bank for me to crawl along. I was on the last dry bit of bank.

But that wasn't what made the sick feeling surge up inside me. There was something else floating on the water along with the snowflakes.

It was a hat.

A Leeds United bobble hat.

Seventeen

I shouted out, "Kenny! Kenny!" as loud as I could. Stupidly, I aimed my shouts at the hat, as if he were walking along under the surface, with just the hat sticking up out of the water. Tina whined and barked and whined, and moved in a small circle.

I tried to drag myself out there, but the water was too deep, soon up over my arms. The icy chill of it paralysed me, so I had to get back to my sliver of dry rock.

I screamed out again with frustration and pain and loneliness. The images of what might have happened flowed through my brain, like I was watching a load of YouTube videos. Kenny making it this far, getting stuck, not wanting to come back without having completed his mission, trying to wade on. The water getting higher, freezing him. Up to his waist, his neck. Kenny stumbling, taking in that fatal mouthful of water – just as I'd imagined doing myself. Frozen and drowned.

I tried to make better videos play. Kenny somehow skirting this part of the river, making it down to the road. Kenny safe. Rescuers coming for me.

I was shivering now, more than Tina. So cold I couldn't think any more. The gloves were soaked, of course, so they didn't do any good. I took them off and shoved my hands under my armpits. Tina was next to me again. I lay on my side, pulled my legs up and curled around her.

I would have cried, I think, but it turns out you can reach a level of coldness where you can't cry, no matter how sad you are. All you are is cold.

I started to drift again. Memories from when we were small. My mum was there, but I don't know if it was her as she really was or just something my mind invented, made up from mothers I'd seen on the telly or read about in books. She had old-fashioned clothes – a dress with flowers on it, an apron. And her hair was tied up in a bun.

Somewhere else, I remembered my dad staggering around drunk in the kitchen. "Where is it?" Dad was yelling. "Where is it?"

Booze, I suppose he meant.

And I remembered an argument. Mum and Dad screaming at each other. No, not at each other. My dad just slurring a few words; my mum's voice like a machine gun firing icicles. Me and Kenny upstairs, listening on the landing. Then Kenny crying in bed, the pillow over his head. Me telling Kenny a story. Maybe it was the first story I ever told him. One I'd heard at school. What story? Hansel and Gretel. The trail of bread. The two children left in the forest ... No, I wouldn't have told him that one. I wasn't that stupid. Maybe it was the Little Mermaid, as I've got a memory somewhere of Kenny murmuring, "Mermaid, mermaid ..."

Tina was cold next to me. She was a good dog. Well, she wasn't clever and she didn't do any tricks, but she loved Kenny. Good isn't the same as clever.

I tried to warm Tina up. Wrapped myself more tightly around her.

I put my lips next to her wet head and spoke to her. What did I say? I don't know. The words you say to dogs. She put her tongue out and curled it upwards to try to lick my face. The tip of it touched my nose. It was rough and dry.

The water was still rising. I had my back to the stone wall of the gorge now. But I didn't care any more about drowning. I didn't want to be alive without Kenny, knowing that I'd sent him to die in the cold water.

And then I remembered something else. Something to do with one of those stories. Another sad one. A small girl selling matches on the streets. Imagine that, someone so poor they had to sell matches? But she's so cold and so lonely she lights the matches, and the light of the flames makes her less sad.

Why was that story in my head? The ending wasn't happy ...

Matches.

LIGHTER!

I had my mum's old lighter. In the inside pocket of my jacket. I reached in there with fingers as numb as stone. I found it. I turned the wheel with my thumb twice, and only sparks came. The third time the flame caught. The gold and blue of the burning gas was as bright as the sun, and the most beautiful thing I'd ever seen. I put my frozen fingers almost in the flame, and my fingers ate the warmth. Before I burned myself, I changed hands, letting the flames dance around my other fingers.

"Here, Tina, come, try to get warm," I said to the little dog. But all she could do was turn her head to look at me for a second before she slumped down again.

After a minute, the metal at the top of the lighter grew too hot to hold. I let go of the plastic button that kept it alight.

Suddenly the world became black. Blacker than it had been before. And I was as scared now of the black as I was scared of the cold and the rising water. I struck the lighter again and lived off its flame for another two minutes. I struck it for a third time and I thought that the flame was thinner, smaller. When I let it go out, I put the hot lighter in between my jumper and my T-shirt. That was glorious, for a few seconds.

The fourth time, the flame lasted for less than a minute. Then it died, and the darkness was everywhere, and I lost all my hope.

Eighteen

It was the morning. Light filled the gorge. Pale
blue light with golden lines in it, like rays of the
sun drawn by a little kid. And then the rock of the
gorge opened out, like a scallop shell, or like a book.
Or like when you're holding a butterfly, and you
show your friend, your dark-haired girlfriend, and
she comes over and you open your hands. And the
butterfly – nothing special, only a cabbage white –
spreads its wings and flutters them, making sure
they still have power in them, and then it's away
into the blue and gold air. And I was lying on my
back, gazing up, watching the soft white lines in
the sky. Remembering what my dad said – that
when he was a kid, before the internet, when there
was nowt on the telly during the day, him and his
friends used to watch the white contrails for hours

in the endless blue of summer skies, just like me and Kenny watching the telly. And Kenny was here. That was good. I couldn't see him, but he was here. And Sarah. I knew if I turned my head she'd be there, too. I reached out, trying to find a hand, thinking it would be Sarah or Kenny, but I could only feel the soft hay we were lying on. The hay of the field near the wood where the badgers lived.

And then I heard the sound. The mad, ecstatic music of the lark. I peered into the brightness and saw the small bird straining upwards, its flight not like the easy, carefree swooping of the swallows and swifts. The lark's flight was all effort, as if hauling itself up by sheer will – a wanting, a yearning. To fly and to sing was work, it was grit. And it was beautiful. And then the lark flew so high it escaped the earth's gravity, and suddenly flying was no effort at all. And finally the lark was so high that I lost the song, and though I tried to keep my eye on the tiny dot in the blue forever, striving to keep my eyes open in case I couldn't find it again, at last I blinked, and my eyes opened not into the blue and gold but into the black.

And then I understood that the lark wasn't a lark, but a soul, and that I was alone, and that a beautiful thing had left this world.

Nineteen

"Listen to me. Nicky. You're OK. Can you hear me? Look at me."

Lines of light were playing about the gorge. Like searchlights in the war.

There was a man. He had a yellow helmet on. A torch in the helmet. I'd always wanted one of those. He had a moustache. Who had a moustache these days?

I didn't understand.

"Kenny," I said.

"Kenny?" the man asked. "Is that your brother?"

"Yeah."

"Kenny's fine."

Other men were there. Not just men. There was a woman. They all had the helmets with the torches, and scratchy clothes. They were doing things to me.

"On three," someone said. "One, two ..." And then rotten pain, the worst for ages. They'd lifted me into something.

They wrapped me up in tin foil.

"You're the world's biggest turkey," someone said.

"Where's Kenny?" I asked.

"He's waiting for you."

"Is he dead?"

"No, lad! Hospital. Hypothermia. But he's fine. Watching the telly, I expect."

All the time the people were working, doing things. Straps. Grunting.

Someone said, "Let's get him out of here while we still bloody can."

I turned my head and saw Tina still lying on the rock.

"My dog," I said.

But I already knew.

"I'm sorry, son," the man said.

"Don't leave her."

"Wouldn't dream of it."

"Will you bury her? Somewhere nice ..."

"Course I will."

"Don't tell Kenny," I said.

"Course not."

They were lifting me. The men and the woman. Carrying me. I strained back my head to see. The man picked up Tina, our dog, who had given up the last of her warmth to me.

It always feels like cheating in a story when people black out and wake up later. Well, I didn't black out. I remember being carried back along the gorge, the men and the woman sometimes splashing in the water, sometimes climbing over the rocks. And then we went up, the rescue people grunting as they tried to keep the stretcher level. And then it became easier, and then we were at the road, and an ambulance was waiting with its light flashing blue. All the time I cried for Tina, with sadness, and for Kenny, with relief. And I cried a bit because my fucking leg hurt so much.

It took ages to get to the hospital, the ambulance going along the narrow roads. But I didn't mind. I was warm. Then we got there, and there was a big fuss when I got in. The lights of the hospital were too bright. Nurses checking things, doctors checking things. It was only then that I realised the man who'd picked up Tina wasn't there.

I wanted to thank him, and the others. Maybe I had, I couldn't remember.

The first thing they did was to wash my face and put a bandage on my head. I'd forgotten that I'd bashed it when I fell. Then they wheeled me in to have my leg X-rayed. A doctor told me they couldn't put a cast on it till the next day, as they had to wait for the swelling to go down. They gave me tablets that made the pain go away. Other things happened. Then my dad was there, and Jenny. It was still the night time.

"Sorry, Dad," I said.

My dad had wet eyes.

"Daft bugger," he said. I think he was talking to himself.

Then I was on a trolley being wheeled around the hospital, with Dad on one side and Jenny on the other.

"Are we going to Kenny?" I asked.

"Aye," Dad said.

"And he's OK?"

"You'll see."

"How do you know he's OK?"

"We've already been in to see him," said Jenny. "He's good." Jenny wasn't our mum, but I loved her.

And then we got to where Kenny was. It was a ward with five beds in it, and Kenny was in one. He was watching the telly, but with no sound on.

"All right, our Nicky," Kenny said. "I was worried. But they said they'd get you. I freezed me knackers off. Tina didn't like it when the water got deep, so she ran back to you. I lost my hat. A doctor said he'd get me a new one. I said Man City not Leeds. Leeds are rubbish. What have they done to your leg?"

"They fixed it up," I said. "They'll put a cast on it tomorrow and you can sign it."

Kenny loved writing his name. He put his own special swirls and loops on all the letters.

"They said it was too late to have the sound on the telly," Kenny told me. "So I was just watching the pictures. Where's Tina? Do they not let dogs in the hospital? Is it cos they've got germs?"

Kenny didn't look at me but kept his face towards the small TV screen.

I knew what I was going to say. I'd practised it in the ambulance.

"Tina loved it there, on the moors. She didn't want to come back to our town. There was a farmer waiting when we got to the road. He said that Tina could go to his farm, and he'd train her to be a sheepdog. The farmer said it was the best life for a dog, with all the walks she wanted and other dogs to play with. He said it was heaven for a dog."

Kenny's face was pale in the light from the telly. I could tell that he was imagining Tina there on the farm, herding the sheep and playing with the other sheepdogs.

"Yeah," Kenny said. "I'm tired." The remote for the telly was on the bed. He picked it up and turned the screen off. "I'm glad you're OK, our Nicky."

"Only thanks to you, Kenny," I said. "You saved me. You're a hero."

It wasn't until then that I realised he had on his Spiderman pyjamas. Jenny must have brought them for him. Dad would never have thought of it.

They put me in the bed next to Kenny's. I could reach out and touch him. Dad and Jenny went home. It was dark in the hospital, but nurses still moved about quietly, their shoes making almost no sound. Kenny was asleep, his long arms and his big hands outside the covers. I reached out and took his hand in mine.

"Tell me a story," Kenny murmured.

And so I told him about Tina on the farm, and the time she saved the sheep from the gytrash, and how the farmer gave her sausages as a reward. Then the Queen came to give Tina a medal, and she got married to one of the Queen's corgis and spent half the year in Buckingham Palace and half on the farm.

If I'm honest, it wasn't my best story ever.

Twenty

A week later, we were at Manchester Airport. Me and Kenny had never been to an airport before. He loved everything about it, the escalators and the shops, and the way everything was shiny.

And then we got to the area with big windows that looked out over the planes ready to take off. Kenny pressed his face against the glass and gawped. I gawped a bit, too. Stupid, I know, two teenagers staring at aeroplanes like they'd just been invented. But we'd never seen one this close before. Mixed up with the beauty of everything, and the excitement of so many people around us, and all the new things, there was also a bit of sadness in me. Not just sadness. Anger at the unfairness of it all. Because I'd seen so little in my life. Never even been out of Yorkshire before this drive to Manchester. And for the first time ever, I wanted to go away, to fill my eyes with the new. To have something different to look at every day ...

But we weren't here to look at planes and think about escaping.

Me and Kenny and Dad were here to meet my mum. I was in a wheelchair, my leg stuck out like a cannon. A shit cannon made from plaster. Kenny had signed it. Some of my mates from school had come round and scribbled on it. Some had drawn knobs, which I changed into Norman soldiers. (That's a good tip, if someone draws a knob on your exercise book.) And Sarah had written her name ...

To begin with, Kenny had pushed my wheelchair around the airport. But then he got too excited about everything else, so now it was my dad.

We got to the arrivals hall and waited.

"Plane's on time," my dad said.

He was wearing the nearest thing he owned to a suit. Well, it was two suits, really. The jacket from one suit and the trousers from another. He'd combed his hair. I noticed that Dad was going grey at the sides and his hair was a bit thin on top. But he looked pretty good, for an old feller.

Kenny had on smart new jeans and a sweatshirt from Gap.

The arrivals hall was filled with light from the big windows. There were dozens of people there, waiting to meet passengers off the flight, like us. Lots of them were taxi drivers holding up names written on cardboard. But there were some other families – mums and dads and kids.

"You OK, Nicky?" my dad asked. He put his hand on my shoulder.

"Yeah," I told him.

And then I said something I'd never said before.

"I love you, Dad."

I felt my dad's hand tighten on my shoulder.

"Because, Dad, you were always ... you never went ... away."

"No, Nicky," Dad said, his voice thick. "I went away. It was you who stayed. It was you ..."

"It was us, Dad, us," I said.

And then I heard a noise from Kenny. It was a mix of a laugh and a cry and a shout of joy and a groan of pain. And then, in the light that was so bright I had to half shut my eyes, I saw her ...

Epilogue

And the years went by. Forty of them, and I was here again in the hospital with Kenny.

Mum and Dad were gone. Jenny was still Jenny. She hardly looked different, but she was a little old lady now.

I'd been in the room with Kenny for six hours. They told me he didn't have long. He was asleep for most of the time. Twice he woke up and looked at me, and I took his hand in mine – as I had all those years ago, when he'd saved me. He was bald, Kenny, from the chemo. But he was going bald anyway. A bit of fuzz had grown back on his head after they'd stopped the treatment. It was so soft it was hard to resist the urge to stroke it.

They loved their uncle Kenny, my two kids. He'd never got tired of playing with them when they'd been small.

"Do horsy, Uncle Kenny!" they'd squeal, and they'd both ride around on his long back.

He'd had their names, Ruth and Stan, tattooed on his knuckles.

Kenny had loved his job at the garden centre. He'd always wanted to work with animals, but that had never happened, and plants were the next best thing.

I think his life had been happy.

Happier than mine? Maybe. I was OK. Me and Sarah had our ups and downs, but we were still together. Teaching was hard work, but it was good when you saw some snotty-nosed scamp in Year 7 growing up and getting four A levels and going off to uni.

Kenny opened his eyes again. This time they focused on me, rather than into the world beyond.

"Did Tina really go to the farm to be a sheepdog?" Kenny said, his voice just a sigh.

I hadn't thought about our little Jack Russell for years. I thought about lying to Kenny now, but I couldn't, not at the end.

"No, Kenny," I said. "Tina kept me warm until the mountain rescue team found us. She gave up all her warmth for me."

Kenny's breathing carried on for a while.

"You shouldn't have told me a lie, Nicky."

"I know, brother," I said. "But I didn't want you to be sad."

Breathing, breathing.

"Will Tina be in heaven?" Kenny asked.

"I think she will, yeah."

"And will I see her there?"

"Course you will, Kenny."

"How will I find her?"

"You won't have to," I said. "She'll come and sniff you out when you get there."

Breathing, breathing. Softer. Kenny's eyes were almost closed.

"Nicky?" he murmured.

"Yeah?"

"All our adventures ... Snuffy and Rooky, and when we got that watch off that man who was drowned ..."

"Yeah. I remember," I said. "I remember all of them. They're not the sort of things you forget."

"You always said you'd write them down. Get them made into a book."

I had said that. I'd told my kids all about the stuff we'd got up to, me and their uncle Kenny. But I'd never had the time to sit down and write it all out.

"I've been … busy, Kenny. Life gets filled up with stuff."

"Promise me you will," Kenny said.

"What?"

"Write it all."

"Aye, Kenny, I will."

"You've got to promise."

"I promise."

Kenny's eyes were closed now, but he nodded.

And then his last words, so faint I could hardly hear them. Yet in another way so loud that they rang out like the ecstatic song of the lark in the endless blue sky.

"Tell me a story."

Acknowledgements

My thanks, as ever, to the brilliant
Barrington Stoke team, most particularly
Ailsa Bathgate and Jane Walker.

Thanks also to Charlie Campbell for
doing my deals.

The first three instalments of Nicky and Kenny's story
are now available in a beautiful combined edition:

ISBN: 9781781128466